TYRANNOSAURUS DRIP

About the author and illustrator:

Julia Donaldson has written some of the world's favourite picture books. She also writes books for older children, as well as plays and songs, and she spends a lot of time on stage performing her brilliant sing-along shows! Julia has wanted to write a story about a small dinosaur ever since she was a child and learnt that most dinosaurs were actually the size of a hen.

David Roberts designed hats before he started illustrating children's books. Since then he has illustrated many books which have sold all over the world – and he's won awards for them too! David used to have a cat called Eugene who looked like a furry Stegosaurus.

CALGARY PUBLIC LIBRARY

JUN   2013

For Suzanne Carnell and Chris Inns

First published 2007 by Macmillan Children's Books
This edition published 2013 by Macmillan Children's Books
a division of Macmillan Publishers Limited
20 New Wharf Road, London N1 9RR
Basingstoke and Oxford
Associated companies throughout the world
www.panmacmillan.com

ISBN: 978-1-4472-3490-6

Text copyright © Julia Donaldson 2007
Illustrations copyright © David Roberts 2007
Moral rights asserted

All rights reserved. No part of this publication may be reproduced, stored in or introduced
into a retrieval system, or transmitted, in any form, or by any means (electronic, mechanical,
photocopying, recording or otherwise) without the prior written permission of the publisher.
Any person who does any unauthorised act in relation to this publication may be liable to
criminal prosecution and civil claims for damages.

2 4 6 8 9 7 5 3 1

A CIP catalogue record for this book is available from the British Library.

Printed in China

TYRANNOSAURUS DRIP

Julia Donaldson

Illustrated by David Roberts

MACMILLAN CHILDREN'S BOOKS

In a swamp beside a river,
    where the land was thick with veg,
Lived a herd of duckbill dinosaurs
    who roamed the water's edge.

And they hooted, "Up with rivers!"
    and they hooted, "Up with reeds!"
And they hooted, "Up with bellyfuls
    of juicy water weeds!"

Now across the rushy river, on a hill the other side,
Lived a mean Tyrannosaurus
    with his grim and grisly bride.
And they shouted, "Up with hunting!"
    and they shouted, "Up with war!"
And they shouted, "Up with bellyfuls
    of duckbill dinosaur!"

But the two Tyrannosauruses, so grisly, mean and grim,
Couldn't catch the duckbill dinosaurs
    because they couldn't swim.
And they muttered, "Down with water!"
    and they muttered, "Down with wet!"
And they muttered, "What a shame
    that bridges aren't invented yet."

Now a little Compsognathus
    (but for short we'll call her Comp)
Found a duckbill egg and stole it
    from a nest beside the swamp.

And she swam with it,

and ran with it,

And murmured, "Clever me!"
And, "Won't the baby Comps
be thrilled with
duckbill egg for . . .

"…T!"

She dropped the egg in terror
    and went running for her life
From the mean Tyrannosaurus
    and his grim and grisly wife.

And the duckbill egg went rolling,
    and at last it came to rest
In — of all unlikely places —
    the Tyrannosaurus nest.

Now the mother T had great big jaws
    and great enormous legs,
But her brain was rather little
    and she couldn't count her eggs.
And she sang, "Hatch out, my terrors,
    with your scaly little tails
And your spiky little toothies
    and your scary little nails."

Out hatched Babies One and Two,
  as perfect as could be,
But Mother T was horrified by
  Baby Number Three.
And she grumbled, "He looks weedy,"
  and she grumbled, "He looks weak."
And she grumbled, "What long arms —
  and look, his mouth is like a beak!"

"He just needs feeding up," said Dad
    and gave the babes some meat.
The first two gulped and guzzled
    but the third refused to eat.
And he said, "I'm really sorry,"
    and he said, "I simply can't."
And he said, "This meat looks horrible.
    I'd rather eat a plant."

"A PLANT!" yelled Mum in horror,
    and Dad said, "Get a grip!"
His sisters found a name for him:
    "Tyrannosaurus Drip!"
And they shouted, "Up with hunting!"
    and they shouted, "Up with war!"
And they shouted, "Up with bellyfuls
    of duckbill dinosaur!"

Poor Tyrannosaurus Drip
    tried hard to sing along
But the others yelled, "You silly drip,
    you've got the words all wrong!"
For he hooted, "Down with hunting!"
    and he hooted, "Down with war!"
And he hooted, "Down with bellyfuls
    of duckbill dinosaur!"

Drip's sisters soon grew big enough
  to hunt with Dad and Mum
But they turned on Drip and told him,
  "You're not fierce enough to come."

And he cried, "They've gone without me!"
  and he cried, "Alackaday!"
And he cried, "This doesn't feel like home.
  I'm going to run away!"

So he ran off to the river,
  where he saw a lovely sight:
A herd of duckbill dinosaurs,
  all hooting with delight.
And they hooted, "Up with rivers!"
  and they hooted, "Up with reeds!"
And they hooted, "Up with bellyfuls
  of juicy water weeds!"

As he stood there on the bank,
  a sudden urge took hold of him,
And he jumped into the water . . .
  and discovered he could SWIM!
And the duckbills came to greet him
  by the rushy river's edge
And they hooted, "Nice to see you!"
  and they hooted, "Have some veg!"

And Drip, who was delighted
that they hadn't run away,
Ate bellyfuls of water weeds,
and played with them all day.

Then he gazed into the river
    and he asked them, "Who, oh who
Is that creature in the water?"
    And they laughed and said, "It's you!"

That night the lightning crackled
and a storm blew down a tree.
And it fell across the river,
and the Ts cried out, "Yippee!"

And they shouted, "Up with hunting!"
and they shouted, "Up with war!"
And they shouted, "Up with bellyfuls
of duckbill dinosaur!"

Drip's sisters stepped onto the bridge,
but then began to frown,
For there in front of them stood Drip,
who yelled, "Look out! Look DOWN!"

And they looked into the water,
    and they each let out a yelp,
And one cried, "Water monsters!"
    And the other one cried, "HELP!"

Their mother scolded, "Nonsense!"
and she joined them on the tree.
Then she looked into the water and
exclaimed, "Good gracious me!"

The three of them stood trembling,
and Dad said, "Get a grip!
You're all of you as drippy as
Tyrannosaurus Drip!"

He strode onto the bridge and scoffed,
"I bet there's nothing there."
Then he looked into the water —

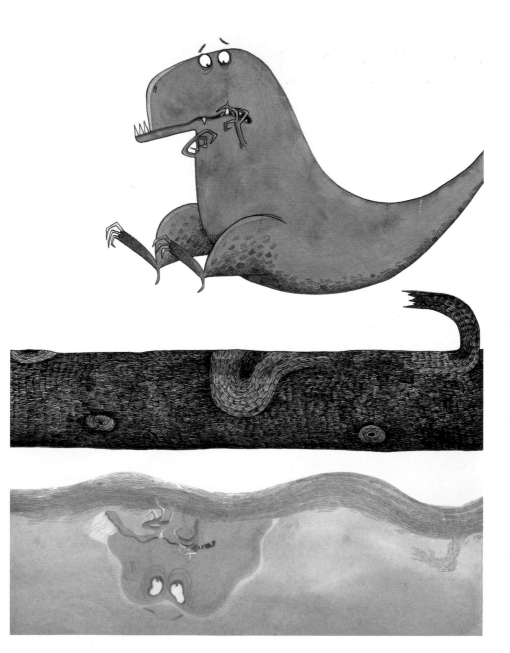

and he jumped into the air.

And how the duckbills hooted
when he landed with a crash,
And the tree bridge broke . . .

. . . and four
Tyrannosauruses went

SPLASH!

And spluttering, and clinging to
the branches of the tree,
They went whooshing down a waterfall
and all the way to sea.

And the duckbills hooted happily:
they hooted, "Hip hip hip . . .
Hooray for the heroic,
one-and-only Duckbill Drip!"

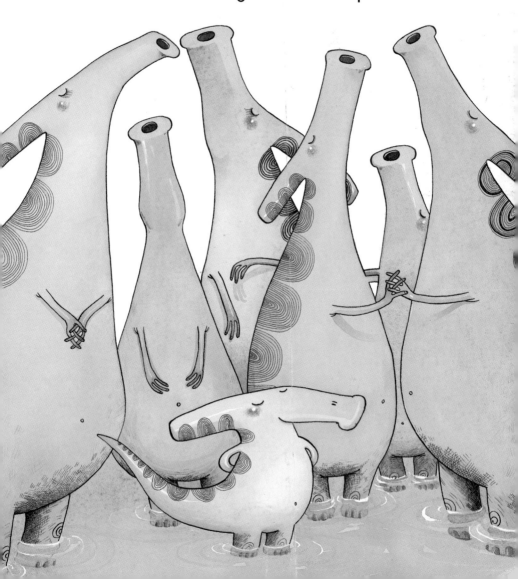